MYSTERY ON THE LEGO EXPRESS

By Trey King
Illustrated by Sean Wang

SCHOLASTIC INC.

ISBN 978-0-545-60366-9

10 9 8 7 6 5 4 3 2 1
Printed in the U.S.A.

14 15 16 17 18 19/0
40

First printing, September 2014

Designed by Angela Jun

"Please hurry!" Mr. Clue says to the taxi driver. He doesn't want to be late for his train. Today he is going on a much-needed vacation.

Mr. Clue runs through the train station. His mouth waters when he smells the yummy food nearby. But there's no time for food—he needs to get on that train!

"Whew!" Mr. Clue sighs. He made it to the train *just* in time. The whistle sounds as the train pulls out of the station. His vacation has officially started, and it's time to relax. But as he closes his eyes to take a nap . . .

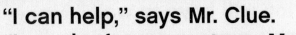

"I can help," says Mr. Clue.

"I am the famous actress Marilyn Money, and someone has stolen my golden award statue!" the woman cries.

"I see. Please tell me everything," says the clever detective.

"It wasn't me!" the boxer growls. "I bet *you* did it!"
"No way!" the cowgirl yells. "It was probably *him*!"
Everyone is arguing and pointing at one another.
Mr. Clue had better solve this crime quickly before
people get really upset.

While all of the passengers are fighting, Mr. Clue gets to work. He uses his magnifying glass to check the scene of the crime. The actress's seat offers a lot of clues.

"Every person in this train car left something at the scene of the crime. It would seem that *ALL* of you are suspects," says Mr. Clue. "So, tell me, why were each of you near the gold statue?"

I thought the award was one of my gold teeth. Then I remembered my gold teeth are *in* my mouth.

I would never steal anything—except maybe a pony!

It was so pretty, I just wanted to hold it for a minute. But I put it back when I was done.

I was just comparing her award to my trophy, and mine is bigger! Football rules!

If I wanted a gold statue, I would just buy one. I'm *really* rich.

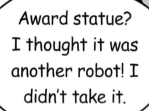

I thought it was an alien. But don't worry, it wasn't . . .

Award statue? I thought it was another robot! I didn't take it.

WHAT'S THAT, SONNY? I CAN'T HEAR YOU. WHAT AWARD? GIVE ME BACK MY NEWSPAPER!

"But if all of you are innocent, then that leaves only *one* suspect," says Mr. Clue. "Where is the *farmer*?"

Everyone turns just in time to see the farmer exit the train car.

"Stop, in the name of the law!" Mr. Clue shouts as he follows the farmer to the top of the train. "You need to return what you've taken!"

The wind and train are so loud, the farmer doesn't hear the detective.

"This is supposed to be my vacation, *not* another dangerous chase," Mr. Clue whispers as he moves carefully across the train. "I do *not* like this at all!"

The detective sneaks up behind the farmer before shouting, "You are under arrest, thief!"

"*Huh?*" says the farmer, startled. He accidentally squirts milk into Mr. Clue's face.

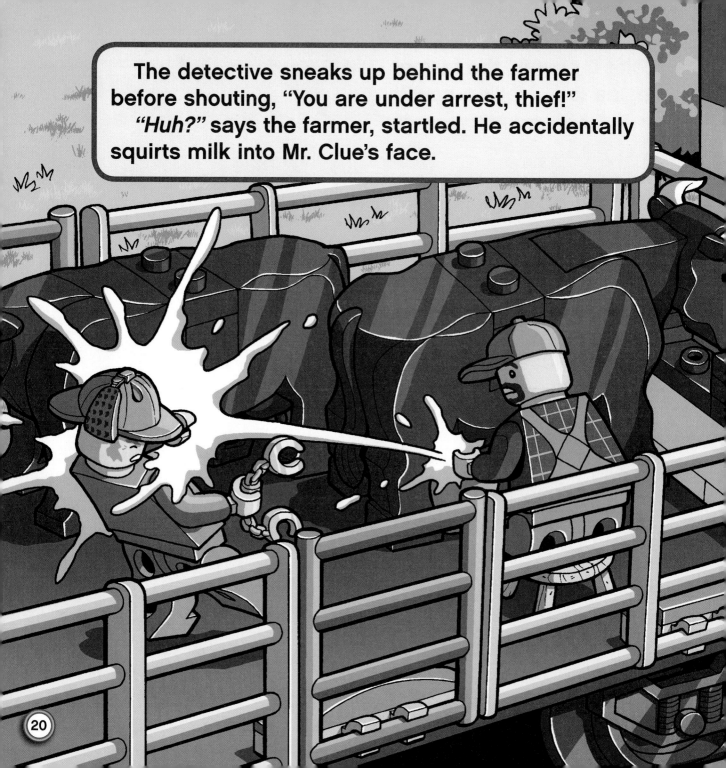

"Sorry about that, mister!" the farmer says. "I came out here to milk my cows. I thought some cookies and milk would help everyone calm down. Did you ever find that statue?"

"You mean *you* don't have it?" asks Mr. Clue. "Then, where is it?!"

Inside the train car, Marilyn Money looks inside her purse. *"Uh-oh!"* she says. "It appears the award was in my purse this whole time."

Now that the crime has been solved and all the excitement is over, Mr. Clue can finally take his nap and start his well-deserved vacation.